THIS BLOOMSBURY BOOK
BELONGS TO

....

At the weekend Mum, Dad and I
visited Planet Earth. I wanted to
see a real live human.

Dad had even lent me
his camera so I could
take a photo of one.

We landed at the zoo because
that's where Mum said all sorts
of earth animals lived.

'HEY, is that a human, Mum?'

'No, son, that's a kangaroo.
Humans don't hop about,
they walk.'

'What about this?
Is this a human, Dad?'

'No, that's a tiger.
Humans don't have tails.'

'What about these, are they humans?'

'No, they're penguins. Humans don't have wings or webbed feet.'

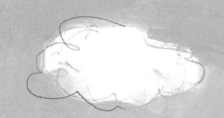

'Up there, that really TALL one.
Is that a human?'
'No, that's a giraffe.
Humans aren't that tall.'

We'd searched nearly the whole zoo.

There was only one cage left . . .

'It's got no tail,
webbed feet or wings.
It isn't really TALL.
It doesn't hop.
Is this a human, Dad?

Is it? Is it? IS IT?'

YES, IT IS!
IT COULD DO WITH A HAIRCUT, THOUGH!
ALIENS' GUIDE TO EARTH

I set up Dad's camera
and took my photo.

And here is my photo of a real live
human being!

Acclaim for this book

'*The Photo* could accurately be described as
an anarchic animal identification book.'
Parents News

'Toddlers will enjoy this wacky tale with odd-looking
aliens and a hilarious case of mistaken identity.'
Junior

'Layton's illustrations, which look as if they were
inspired by children's paintings, have great charm.'
The Daily Telegraph